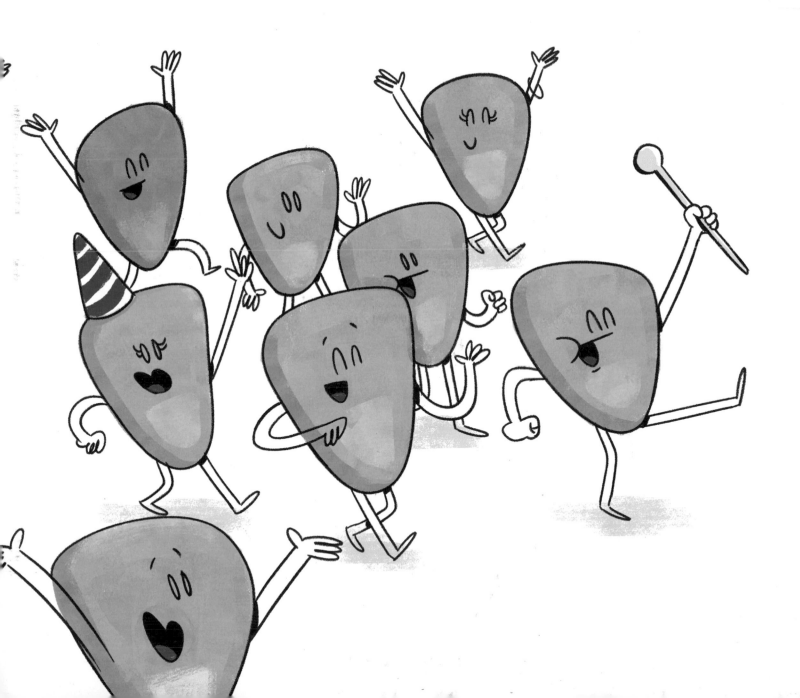

TO DAD, FOR EVERYTHING -KK
TO MY POP, WHO ALWAYS ENCOURAGED ME TO DRAW -GB

GENIUS CAT BOOKS

Genius Cat

WWW.GENIUSCATBOOKS.COM

ABOUT THIS BOOK
THE ART FOR THIS BOOK WAS CREATED WITH PHOTOSHOP AND ILLUSTRATOR, USING A WACOM CINTIQ. TEXT WAS SET IN BEBAS NEUE,
MAGALLANES AND CHAUNCY PRO. IT WAS DESIGNED BY GERMÁN BLANCO.

LIBRARY OF CONGRESS CONTROL NUMBER: 2020952954

ISBN: 978-1-938447-22-8 (HARDCOVER)

FIRST EDITION, 2021

OUR BOOKS MAY BE PURCHASED IN BULK FOR PROMOTIONAL, EDUCATIONAL, OR BUSINESS USE. FOR MORE INFORMATION, OR TO SCHEDULE AN
EVENT, PLEASE VISIT GENIUSCATBOOKS.COM.

PRINTED AND BOUND IN CHINA.

WORDS
KAREN KILPATRICK

PICTURES
GERMÁN BLANCO

POP!

It was a big day.

The Kernels were leaving their jars for the first time to head to the MicroWave!

Otto was ready.

Like the rest of the Kernels, he'd been preparing for this moment.

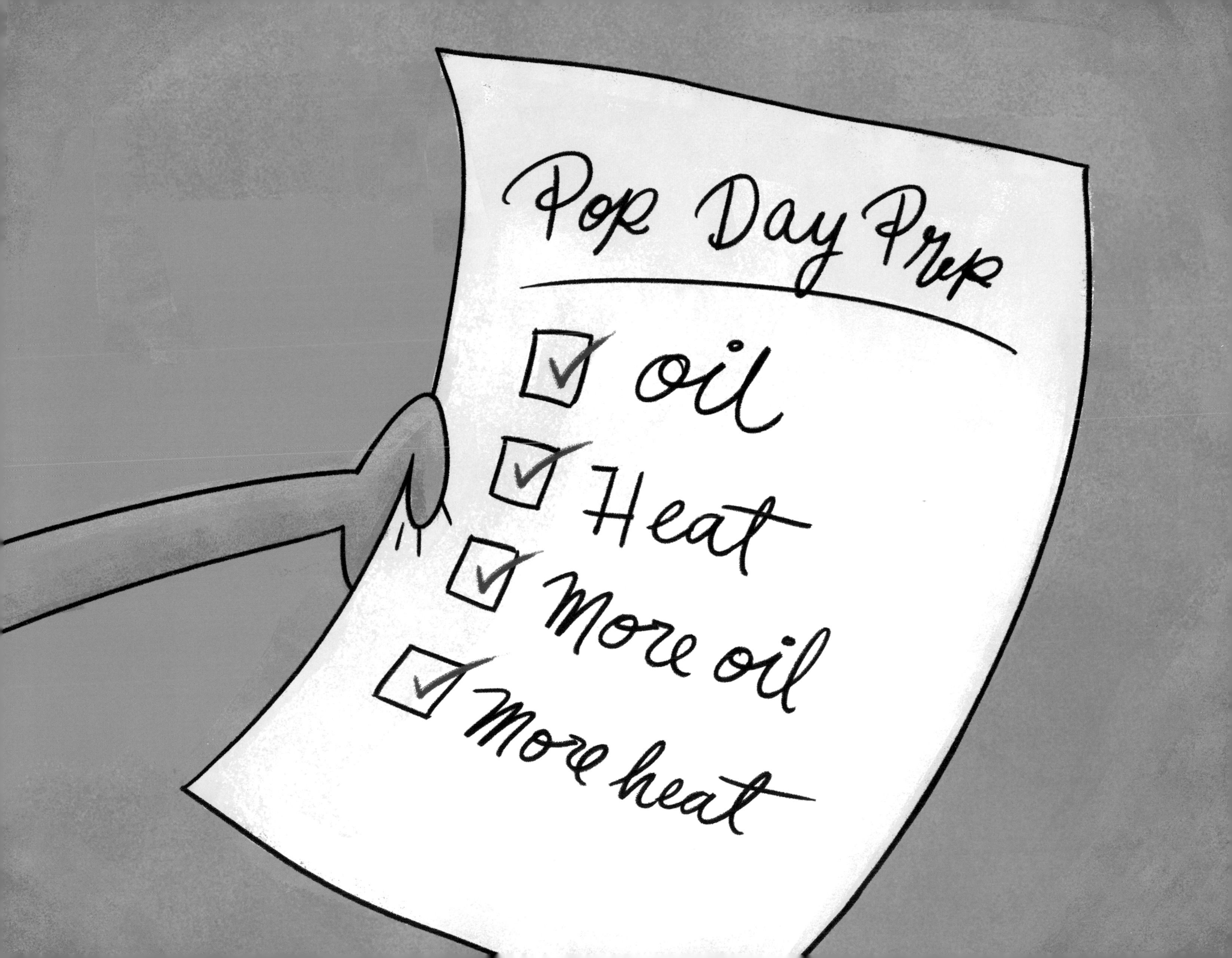
Pop Day Prep
oil
Heat
More oil
More heat

Otto couldn't wait for his turn! Once he popped, he could finally
do all the fun things he'd been dreaming about from the jar, like...

Swim in big buckets of butter,

and even hang out with some Nuts!

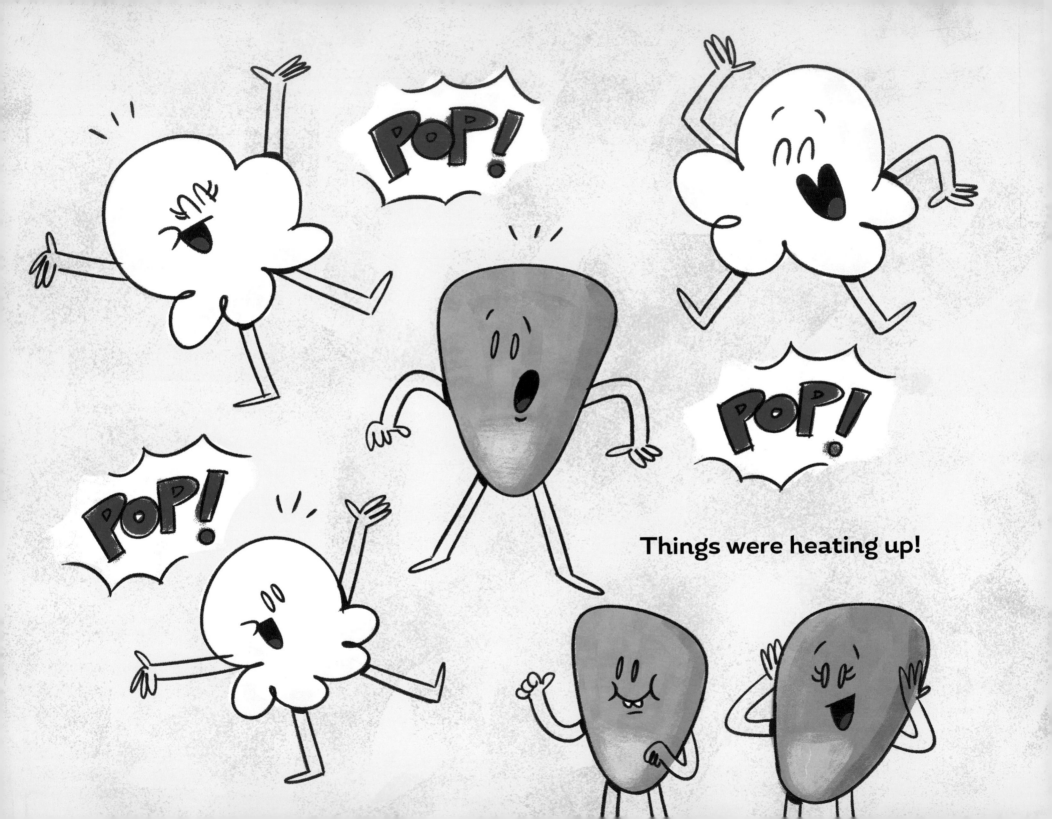

Things were heating up!

All around him, Kernels were becoming popcorn!

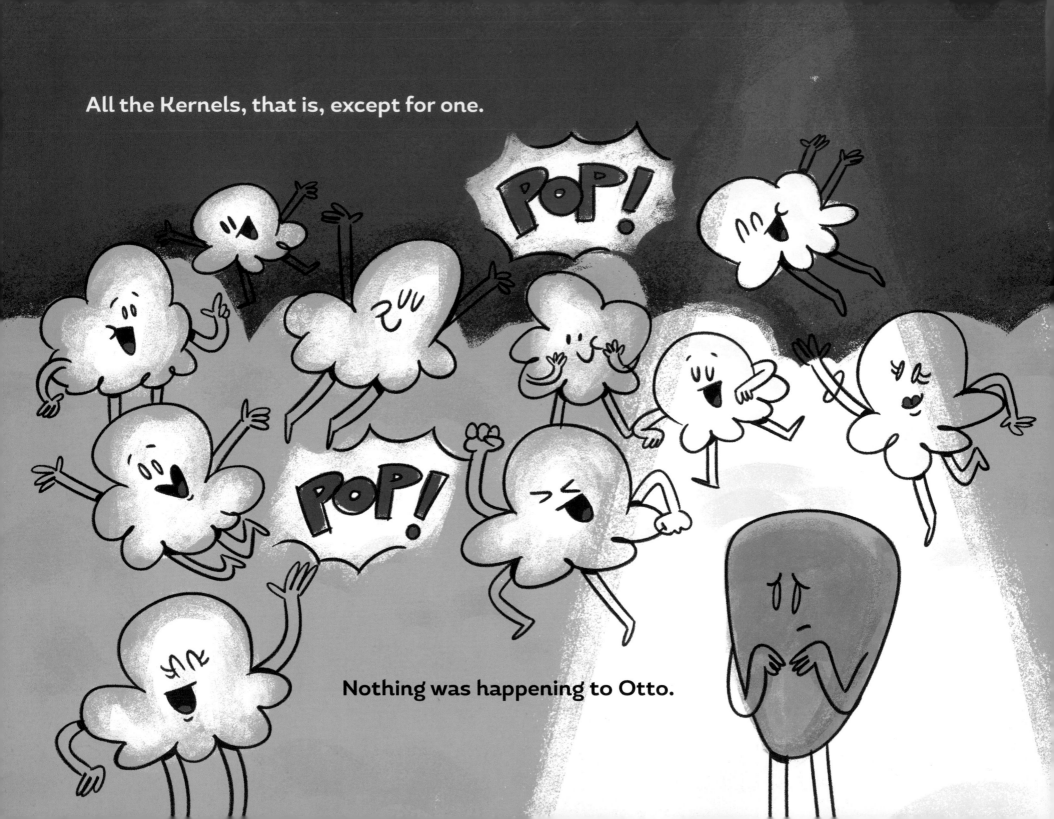

Otto waited until every Kernel had popped. Then waited some more. But Otto never popped.

Did he not use enough oil?

Or get enough heat?

No matter what he tried, Otto remained a Kernel.

While the new Popcorn celebrated,

Otto went back to his jar alone,
where he stayed for a while.

Until one day Otto noticed his favorite smell floating by on the breeze:

butter!

Otto couldn't resist. He followed the delicious smell through the jars, past the MicroWave, and up to a large, yellow bowl.

When Otto peeked inside, he couldn't believe his eyes.

He had thought butter was only for Popcorn!

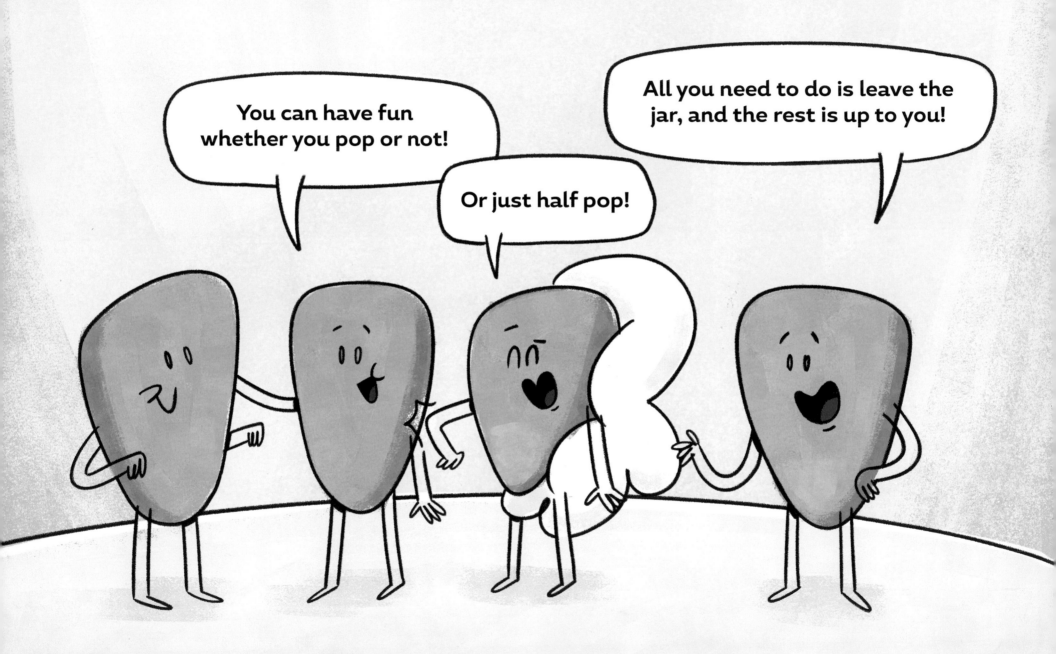

So Otto took a chance.

And you know what?

It was so much fun, it was **NUTS!**

On the next Pop Day, Otto waited outside the MicroWave with a sign.

Just in case there were other Kernels who didn't know that it was okay not to pop.

Dear reader,

We hope you enjoyed reading this book!

You are now officially a member of the **#GeniusCat** family. What does this mean, you ask? Free stuff! Head on over to **GeniusCatBooks.com** for a free eBook and opportunities to receive free physical copies every month. Plus, you can download activities and educator resources, too.

Please join us on Instagram or Facebook:

@geniuscatbooks

We'll do our best to make it fun!

If you purchased this book from a platform where you can leave a review, we would greatly appreciate it if you would provide us with your honest feedback. It helps the book reach more readers, and it makes us feel good (usually!).

Our mission is to help foster a lifelong love of reading through publishing books that entertain, inspire, and educate. We're always happy to hear your feedback on how we are achieving or can better accomplish this goal.

With love,

 Genius Cat Books